THE TAILOR OF GLOSTER

MRS TITTLE-MOUSE

SQUIRREL NUTKIN

TOM KITTEN

PETER RABBIT

FREDERICK WARNE

Published by the Penguin Group
Registered office: 80 Strand, London, WC2R ORL
Penguin Young Readers Group, 345 Hudson Street, New York, N.Y. 10014, USA

First published 1906 by Frederick Warne
This edition with new reproductions of Beatrix Potter's book illustrations first published 2007
This edition copyright © Frederick Warne & Co. 2007
New reproductions of Beatrix Potter's book illustrations copyright © Frederick Warne & Co. 2002
Original copyright in text and illustrations © Frederick Warne & Co., 1906

Frederick Warne & Co. is the owner of all rights, copyrights and trademarks in the
Beatrix Potter character names and illustrations.

Manufactured in China

THE STORY OF
MISS MOPPET

BY BEATRIX POTTER

FREDERICK WARNE

THIS is a Pussy called Miss Moppet,
she thinks she has heard a mouse!

THIS is the Mouse peeping out behind the cupboard, and making fun of Miss Moppet. He is not afraid of a kitten.

THIS is Miss Moppet jumping
just too late; she misses the Mouse
and hits her own head.

SHE thinks it is a very
hard cupboard!

THE Mouse watches Miss Moppet
from the top of the cupboard.

MISS MOPPET ties up her
head in a duster, and sits before
the fire.

THE Mouse thinks she is
looking very ill. He comes
sliding down the bell-pull.

MISS MOPPET looks worse
and worse. The Mouse comes
a little nearer.

Miss Moppet holds her poor
head in her paws, and looks at
him through a hole in the duster.
The Mouse comes *very* close.

AND then all of a sudden —
Miss Moppet jumps upon
the Mouse!

21

AND because the Mouse
has teased Miss Moppet
— Miss Moppet thinks
she will tease the Mouse;
which is not at all nice of
Miss Moppet.

SHE ties him up in the duster,
and tosses it about like a ball.

BUT she forgot about
that hole in the duster;
and when she untied it
— there was no Mouse!

HE has wriggled out and
run away; and he is dancing a
jig on the top of the cupboard!